AFRICAN WRITERS SERIES

Founding editor · Chinua Achebe

Amadu's Bundle

Fulani Tales of Love and Djinns

MALUM AMADU
collected by *GULLA KELL*
and translated into English
by Ronald Moody

HEINEMANN
London · Nairobi · Ibadan

Heinemann Educational Books Ltd
48 Charles Street, London W1X 8AH
P.M.B. 5205 Ibadan · P.O. BOX 25080 Nairobi
EDINBURGH MELBOURNE TORONTO AUCKLAND
NEW DELHI SINGAPORE HONG KONG
KUALA LUMPUR

ISBN 0 435 90118 4

PR
9387.9
A5

Printed in England by
Cox & Wyman Ltd, London, Reading and Fakenham

Contents

Editor's Note

Amadu came from Yola, a fairly large town in the upper Benue in British territory, and like myself he had been kept at Palkumre in the highlands of the Central Cameroons by the rains. After a long conversation, I could no longer restrain my habitual enthnologist's question: 'Have you any stories, poetry or fairy tales?' 'Yes, Madame, I have got them.'

I had dreamed and dreamed for months and months, and almost given up hope of hearing such a reply. After answering my torrent of excited questions, Amadu rose from his mat, and with the kind and soothing expression of a nanny who fetches the beloved toy for her screaming infant, Amadu, who had been practically my neighbour for a whole week, ran through the rain to fetch his books.

He was back in no time with a colossal bundle which seemed at least three feet high and wide. Surely it must contain a whole library! The outer covering was a large discarded hip-cloth of a woman, with each of the four corners tied in a knot, and a long narrow strip of cotton cloth was wound round and round it making a neck with the knots like a face towering above it. It took some time to undo all this and a second cloth appeared with only the corners knotted; then a third and a fourth. I lost count but the middle of the bundle was eventually reached. There, in the heart of this giant onion, was a small parcel of books. It was also tied up in a strip of cotton with many knots which were undone with loving care, and after the Koran and some Arabic texts had been removed, there were revealed some fifty to sixty pages of beautiful and ancient hand-made paper covered in slightly faded handwriting.

Every day he dictated and discussed his texts with me. Apart from the classics, he wrote down fairy tales, riddles and songs existing only in verbal tradition, as well as some of his own essays composed at my request.

GULLA KELL

Courting

A MAN wishing to court a woman goes early to the market and buys twelve kola nuts; then he searches for the finest perfume he can find. Returning to his bachelor hut, he rapidly begins to dress. First, he puts on three or four robes, one over the other; then he pulls on his trousers, puts his tucked black and white striped cap on his head and slips on his embroidered sandals. As a final touch, he puts on his arm the bracelet with the beautifully wrought dagger; then he sets out for her sarē, the compound where she lives.

On arriving there he cautiously tries to find a boy, a little girl, a wizened old woman, or anyone else who will take a message. The chosen messenger goes and says to the woman: 'Someone says you shall come.'

After a display of coyness, she agrees to go with the messenger. Getting up, she puts on her dress of the finest cloth, perfumes herself, and goes to the man. When she reaches him, they sit down together on one mat; thus she signifies that she accepts him.

The woman, whose head is covered with a cloth, does not look at the man, but remains silent and shy. The man addresses her: 'You there!'

The woman nods, and the man says: 'Love has brought me to you, but I am afraid of you.'

The woman replies: 'Don't be afraid. Speak.'

Again the man says: 'You there!'

After she has nodded again, he takes her hand and lifts off the cloth from her head.

'Oh, how beautiful you are!'

She glances at him shyly.

Then he says: 'I love you. Let us make love.'

The woman answers with a soft click of her tongue. The man now puts his hand in his pocket and takes out the kola nuts, he carefully lays them out on the mat, adding to them the bottle of perfume.

This is the end of the overture. Rising, he says: 'I will go home,' and takes his leave.

Later in the day he goes to the market and buys plenty of the best meat for two or three shillings and sends it to the woman. His messenger beckons her: 'Come out of your hut.' He tells her: 'Such and such a man says: "I send you this."' The woman receives the meat and takes it into her hut, rewarding the messenger with money and kola nuts.

Later in the afternoon, the man goes to the woman with three kola nuts. She meets him at the entrance hut; they talk and laugh and chew kola nuts. Then he says: 'Will you come to me?'

'I will come,' she replies.

'Will you come at prayer time?' he urges.

'When the men are away at the Mosque praying the essayi prayer I will come,' she answers.

The man, his heart filled with joy, says goodbye and returns home.

In the evening he lights his lamp; the woman comes to his sarē and he receives her joyfully. They talk for a long time in whispers. Later the man goes out to the village and buys two kola nuts and offers them to his woman. There is no more talking; they lie down and play together until they sleep. Nothing else happens that night.

Before dawn, at the time of the subaha prayer, the woman gets up and returns home. A little later, the man goes and greets her with a single kola nut. After sunrise at the fajiri prayer, the man sends meat, kola nuts and money to her. In the evening the woman comes to her man, he does not go to her. There she finds kola nuts and sweet perfume. They chew kola nuts and perfume each other with the sweet smelling scent and then they make love.

But all women are different.

Some men take a prostitute. She is very bad. She does not love. But a virtuous woman, if a man approaches her, does not go to him however much he tempts her with money, dresses and ornaments, or whatever he gives her. She does not go to a man unless he is very fine, very rich. Only then will she go to him. To a worthless woman – that is, the brazen hussy who invades the bachelor sarē – a man gives nothing, not so much as a needle.

The Beautiful Woman and her Penniless Husband

HERE IS the story of a beautiful woman and her penniless husband. The husband was so poor that he owned nothing besides a little old quiver, whilst the woman had at least her great beauty.

The Yerima – the son of the Lami'do, the chief of the town – was searching for a new mistress. One day he sent his messenger to the beautiful woman. The woman got up at once and went to the Yerima. She agreed to his proposal and so became his mistress.

Very soon afterwards, the son of the judge came to her, because he too was searching for a mistress. His proposal was equally agreeable to her and they did not lose much time. But neither the Yerima nor the son of the judge knew that they were sharing the same mistress.

Some time after this, the husband of the beautiful woman set out on a trading tour. As soon as he had left, she went to the son of the Lami'do and slept with him until the next morning; then she got up and went straight on to the son of the judge. This went on for fifteen days, until her husband returned. As soon as he came home she sent messages to both her lovers, telling them that her husband was back.

The Yerima replied: 'I must have some of the maize porridge you've cooked for your husband today, and I want to eat it before he has tasted it. It is the kind of food I like most of all.' Now, a man who accepts food from a woman is putting himself in the place of her husband, since the wife whose turn it is to sleep with the husband has the privilege of cooking for him. But the woman did not hesitate.

'Tell him he will get it,' she told the messenger.

A little later, the son of the judge sent to the woman saying that though he knew her husband was back, he would like her to come and stay the night. 'Tell him I'll come,' was her reply to the messenger.

That evening, the woman cooked the porridge with the sauce and told her little korgel or slave-girl: 'Take the porridge to my husband. He is outside the hut.'

The korgel quickly carried the bowl of food to the husband and put it on the ground in front of him. The woman followed her but stood behind the matting in the doorway, since a man never eats in the presence of a woman. The men of the neighbourhood came with their food to join the husband and they all sat down in a circle. 'Allah bless you,' he said, looking at the food. He was about to stretch out his hand to take a bit when his wife in the hut exclaimed:

'The korgel is too stupid! I told her to give my husband his porridge, but she must go and take my mother's food and bring it to him!'

The husband heard her and was very shocked, since a man must never eat food cooked by his mother-in-law; to do so would signify that he had an incestuous desire to sleep with her. He quickly dropped the porridge back into the bowl and called the girl to take the food away. The korgel fetched the bowl and returned it to the woman, who ordered her to take some of the other porridge to her husband. As soon as she had done so, the woman said:

'Korgel, take the porridge and sauce which my husband sent back to the Yerima.' The girl did as she was told.

That night the husband came into the saré and went with his wife into her hut. With a very busy air the woman took a pot of fat and massaged her husband's foot. Then they sat down and talked about all that had happened since he went away.

'I must just go to my mother with some things; thieves might get them in our place.'

Astonished, the man protested: 'But it is night.'

Her only reply was: 'Mhm.'

After a pause, the man got up and girded a knife round his waist and said: 'Come along then, let us go.'

'I am not going with you,' she retorted. 'It is out of the question. I want to go alone.'

In the end the man gave in, and his wife took the shortest way to the bachelor hut of the judge's son. She stayed with him until dawn. Then she rose, dressed and started for home. On the way she quietly slipped into her mother's sarē and took a large and small pumpkin bowl. Carrying them in her hand for all to see, she entered her hut and found her husband already sitting up on the bed.

'Why did you stay the whole night with your mother?' he demanded.

'She had such terrible pains in her head. She was in such pain I had to stay the night,' replied the wife.

'Mhm. All right,' was his only reply.

He got up and went to the sarē of his mother-in-law. He made his salaam. She received him, and they greeted each other: 'Did you sleep well? Did you wake up well? Is your body well?' To which she replied: 'Thank you, my child. I feel very well.'

'But didn't you have a very bad headache last night?'

'Tshoi'dum!' (Nonsense) said his mother-in-law. 'I am very well indeed.' Whereupon the man returned to his hut.

Later in the day he went out for a walk in the town. The Yerima saw him and started to laugh and jeer at him, the Lord and Master of the beautiful woman. Then the son of the judge came and joined in, but the man took no notice of them. A few days later, the two young men again met the husband taking a walk. They followed behind him and spat all over the body of the Lord and Master of the beautiful woman. He did nothing. But when he returned home he said to his wife:

'The Yerima and the judge's son spat on me from head to foot; my robe is soiled. Is there any reason why this should happen?'

'Don't speak about it. Keep quiet,' advised his wife, and he did not mention it again.

Some time had passed when the woman said to her husband: 'Today you must set off on a trading tour; but when you have left the town behind you and the sun is exactly above your head, return at once.'

The man took his little old quiver, took leave of his friends, and, after telling everybody he was going on a trading tour, left the town.

His wife then sent to the Yerima telling him to come quickly, as her husband was away. He came at once and they sat together in her hut.

Later she went out and sent for the son of the judge: 'Come quickly,' she implored. 'My husband has gone.'

He too came at once, and found the son of the Lami'do sitting in her hut. Both young men were astonished and stared at each other furiously.

'A! A! It seems we are both your lovers,' exclaimed the Yerima.

'I've never slept with the judge's son. He is only visiting,' she replied.

This soothed the Yerima, and soon the three of them were laughing and chatting in her hut. Suddenly they heard the rattling of the little old quiver of the husband.

'Wai, wai, wai!' cried the woman, beating her breasts. 'I'll take poison. My husband is back. Quick! Get into that large chest over there. If my husband sees you, he will kill you.'

The two young men quickly jumped into the large chest, which had heavy iron bands round it. The woman closed the lid, locking it with a piece of iron.

When the husband entered her hut, he found her quite alone. They sat on the bed and chatted together. Suddenly she said: 'Take that large chest with the iron bands to the market. I want you to sell it for me.'

The husband tried to lift it, but it was too heavy. The woman went out and called three men, and together with her husband they carried it away on their heads. She walked on in front, and they went to the sarē of a very wealthy merchant who came from a town far away.

The woman made her salaam. The merchant came, and after the greetings were over she said:

'I bring you two beautiful pagans, children of slaves of mine, who have belonged to me for a very long time. If you see them you will agree that they are very beautiful slaves.'

'Bring them in. I want to buy them,' said the merchant.

'All right; but you must put them on a slave chain as soon as you let them out,' warned the woman. The men carried the chest into the sarē and opened it. First they caught the Yerima, and round him went the chain – click! Next followed the son of the judge – click! and the merchant and the woman started to bargain. In the end, the merchant gave the woman a very large sum of money for the two young men, and she went home with her freshly acquired wealth. She made her husband a present of many beautiful robes and a huge sum of money.

Much later, she confessed: 'I sold the Yerima and the son of the judge, both of them!'

'Let's run away at once,' cried her husband, who had become very frightened.

'Kai! Run away? No fear. There's no reason for that at all,' retorted the beautiful woman, his wife.

Soon afterwards, the wealthy merchant said that he

had finished his trading in the town and prepared to return home. He put all his slaves in the chain and walked them and his carrier caravan through the town. Everybody saw the Yerima and the judge's son shackled in a slave chain. This news quickly reached the Lami'do and the judge.

The Lami'do went with his court to the merchant and asked: 'Who sold you my son, the Yerima, and the son of the judge?'

'Ask them yourself,' replied the merchant.

The two young men were questioned but refused to speak. The Lami'do then made an offer to the merchant:

'I will give you ten slaves and once more ten. Set our children free.'

The merchant said it was not enough. Only when the ruler was willing to offer twenty and once more twenty slaves for one of the two young men would he let them out of the slave chain. So the Lami'do had to buy the young men at the price that suited the whim of the merchant.

Everybody in the town now pestered the two young men, with: 'Who sold you?'

After a long time they gave it away: 'That beautiful woman over there. She sold us.'

The Lami'do sent for the husband and wife, but the wife told the messenger: 'My husband is not here.' She went alone to the Lami'do.

She found the whole court assembled. The Lami'do asked: 'Where is your husband?'

'My husband?' answered the woman. 'He has not come. This whole affair is my concern alone.'

When the Lami'do questioned further as to why she had sold the two young men, she replied: 'Let them come. They can tell you why.'

They were called, and the ruler asked them: 'Is this the woman who sold you?'

Both of them again refused to speak. Then the woman said: 'Yes, I did sell them.'

At once all the courtiers and everybody else present advised the Lami'do: 'Let sleeping dogs lie. There must be a reason why she sold them. If there was no reason, she certainly would not have done it.'

'Get up and go home,' said the Lami'do, and the woman went home, singing a happy little song.

Later, the judge, the old man, sent the matchmaker, the old pul-woman, to the beautiful wife. The old pul-woman said: 'My child, the judge sends me. I am to tell you that he loves you and would like to come to your hut tonight.'

'Go, tell him my husband is away,' said the beautiful wife. 'Tell him to come.'

The old matchmaker told the judge: 'She says you can come.'

'Is it really true that her husband is away?' asked the judge a little anxiously.

'Mhm,' answered the old matchmaker. 'He is really away'.

'This evening you must go for a walk,' the woman told her husband.

In the evening the man went for a walk. He had hardly left when the beautiful woman heard the 'parrass, parrass' of the sandals of the judge outside. She met the judge in the middle of the sarē, and they went together into her hut. They sat down and were chatting when the woman heard her husband returning, clearing his throat outside her hut.

She beat her breasts and cried: 'Wai, wai, wai! My husband has returned. Quick. Get up! I'll hide you in the big chest.'

The judge sprang up and the woman put him into the chest, closed the lid and locked it, just as her husband came into her hut.

'Who was that with you?' he demanded.

'I've caught the judge himself. Tomorrow I shall sell him,' she answered gleefully.

'Well done!' exclaimed the delighted husband.

The next morning, the two of them dragged the chest out of the hut and carried it to the market. They put it in the middle of the square among all the people. The woman made it known: 'I want to sell the chest, but for not less than a hundred slaves.' Then she left her husband there with the chest and went home.

Meanwhile, the children of the judge could not find their father. They asked his different wives, but they all agreed: 'We haven't seen him since last night.'

But the son of the judge who had himself been sold saw the chest with the iron bands round it in the market and recognized it at once. With a hundred slaves he bought the chest. The carriers lifted it on their heads and took it to the saré of the judge. When the son opened the chest there was his father, who crawled out shamefacedly.

How could it happen that the beautiful woman was able to sell the Yerima, the judge's son and even the judge himself? Only because women are so full of tricks.

The Three Sayings

THERE WAS once a poor young man who was married. When his wife was big with child he could not bear his poverty any longer, so he left his home and set out to seek his fortune. After wandering about for some time, he found a chieftain, a Lami'do, and began to serve him.

Years had passed when one day the young man said to the Lami'do: 'I want to go home.'

The Lami'do gave him three slaves as a reward for his services, and the man started on his way. After walking for thirty-four days through the wilderness, he met an old man with a beard. They walked along together, without exchanging a single word. At last the young man said: 'We don't talk to each other.'

'If you give me a slave, I'll have something to say to you,' replied the bearded old man.

'Take one,' the young man answered.

Then the old man spoke:

'On your journey you will come to a resting-place with a large tree in the middle. Don't sleep under it.'

The next day they walked on again in silence. After a long time, the man observed: 'My father, we don't talk to each other.'

'Child, if you give me a slave, I'll have something to say to you,' returned the old man.

'Take the slave,' the young man replied.

The bearded old man spoke again:

'On your journey you will come to a small river with large stones over which the water rushes. Don't try to cross it, or you will be drowned.'

On the third day, having walked most of the way in

complete silence, the young man at last ventured: 'We don't talk to each other.'

Again the old man spoke: 'Give me your slave and I shall speak a third time.'

'Take him,' said the young man.

Soon afterwards, he took his leave of the bearded old man and walked on alone. Now, without even a slave left, he was just as poor as when he left home many years before.

He soon reached the resting-place with a large tree growing in the middle. He did not rest under it, but under some bushes not far away. At sunset, a great caravan arrived. The people camped on the resting-ground and the owner of the caravan, the merchant, went to sleep under the tree. In the middle of the night a djinn which lived in the tree came and killed him.

In the early dawn, the headman of the caravan awakened the young man and whispered:

'Get up. The merchant is dead, but his servants must not know. I'll give you his clothes and you must ride on his horse.' The young man got up, helped the headman to drag the body from under the tree, and they covered it with leaves. Then the young man put on the dead merchant's clothes and mounted his horse, and the caravan went on its way.

After some time they came to a small river with rapids. The headman said to the young man: 'I'll go and try to ford it.'

The young man agreed, and the headman went into the water and was drowned. The young man ordered the caravan to halt until the swell of water had died down, and guided them through it safely. And so he now became the owner of the caravan.

At last the young man with all his wealth reached home, where he found that his wife had given him a son. The child was nearly a full grown man. Was it his son or was it not his son? The father didn't know. He already had a dagger in his hand to kill the youth when he paused and listened to his heart. A voice said: 'Kill him.'

But another voice, that of the old man with the beard spoke:

'Put the dagger away.'

The man thought about it, as quick as lightning, and decided not to kill his child. That's how it happened: Allah gave the man wealth and preserved his son because he listened to the voice of the old man with a beard.

The Mother and her Son

There was once a youth beloved by all women. They all loved him and they all came to him. Ashee! Even his own mother was in love with him; she yearned for him; she wanted him.

One day, the youth went to 'The Dance of the Women', the festival for choosing a mate. He did not find a woman he liked, so he came home alone in the middle of the night to his hut. Groping his way to his bed, he found a woman lying there. From head to foot she was swathed in cloth.

'Who are you?' he asked, but the woman remained silent.

The youth thought to himself: 'I'll blow on the fire so that I can see her.' The woman quickly stamped out the fire with her foot. Then she began to caress the young man until he too began to fondle her. They made love together. Thus did the woman, his mother, conceive.

At cockcrow, the mother got up and left. She did not want her son to see her; but the youth had taken ashes and knotted them into the seam of the unknown woman's robe, so that when she left the ashes would fall on the ground.

At daybreak, the young man got up and saw the ashes. He followed the trail to the doorway of a hut, the hut of his mother! When he realized this, his heart became as black as night and started to beat as though in a fever. For three days he did not eat. Then he went to his best friend.

'Brother,' he moaned, 'I've slept with my mother. She tricked me into it.'

'You must go away forever,' replied his friend. 'What

you have done is terrible, and it will be unbearable for you if the people get to know about it.'

'Don't tell this to anyone,' the youth implored. 'You are the only person who knows about it.'

'I shall never tell a soul,' swore his friend.

The young man left and went away into the wilderness. As soon as he had gone, his friend told the story to everybody he met, and very soon the whole village knew about it; and by now the mother of the youth was pregnant.

After wandering about for some time, the young man met a pious priest and scribe and told him what had happened. 'Now I've come to you to learn to gain wisdom,' he said. 'I am afraid of my own fate. I don't want to burn in hell.'

'Do you see this stone?' the priest replied. 'It has no blood. Do you see this piece of old, dry wood? It has no leaves. When you die, you will be in hell fire. It is unavoidable.'

'Please let me stay with you and learn,' the youth begged.

'Stay,' answered the priest. 'Between us there is no ill feeling.' So the young man stayed with him, working in the fields and studying the scriptures till he himself became a priest. And this was very good.

Meanwhile, his mother had given birth to a very beautiful little girl. When the child was old enough to run about, her playmates taunted her. 'Didn't your elder brother sleep with your mother? He is your father and your brother as well.'

The little girl used to cry quietly by herself. Over and over again did her playmates tease her.

These words hurt her very much when she was grown up. One day, she became very angry and ran away. For many days she walked from village to village until she finally arrived at the place where her brother lived. There she went into the sarē of the pious priest and stayed with him, but she told nobody why she had run away. After some time, the priest called the youth and said to him:

'Look, God has sent you a woman; marry her.'

The heart of the young man rejoiced. He had longed very much for the beautiful young girl. They married, and the priest gave them a hut and fields. For a time they lived happily, until the young girl became pregnant.

One day, as they were sitting together chatting, her husband asked her:

'Where do you come from?'

'I come from such-and-such a village,' she replied. 'My playmates used to tease me, saying that my mother slept with my elder brother, so that she became pregnant and gave birth to me. This made me very angry and I ran away, walking from village to village, until I met you and we were married.'

Horrified, the young man ran to the priest and repeated what his wife had told him. The priest was deeply upset.

He said: 'When you die, you will be thrown into hell fire because of the evil thing you did with your mother. Through that she became pregnant and gave you a child. Next you marry your own child, who is your sister. Then this young woman, who is your child and your sister, becomes pregnant! Even I, I tremble with fear.'

'I shall go away,' the young man replied.

He went into the depths of the most forlorn wilderness. There he met a lonely old man who held the shaft of a spear in his hand.

The young man told him his story. 'Such are the sins I've committed in this world. You are a wise old man with the wisdom of age; what do you think about it?'

'As truly as blood will never pour out of that rock; as truly as this dry spear shaft will never bear leaves; so will you never get into Paradise,' answered the wise old man.

The youth became full of rage. He ran far away; he

let his hair grow, dressed himself in rags and ground his knife to a razor edge. He became a robber and murderer. Sometimes he killed his victims; sometimes he merely cut their Achilles tendons and stole their goods. He carried on like this for some years.

One day, he was sitting in a tree waiting for his next victim. A youth came walking along the path, singing to himself, and a woman who had run away from her husband came along on the other side. They met.

'Where are you going to?' demanded the youth.

'Nowhere,' the woman answered. 'I am by myself.'

'Come then, let us make love here in the middle of the path,' the youth suggested. He added: 'If you don't I shall kill you.'

The woman refused, and the young man got hold of her and attempted to rape her. But he, the man up in the tree, took an arrow out of his quiver and shot and killed the young man lying with the woman in the middle of the path. Then he said to the woman: 'Get up and run away,' and she did.

The man came down from the tree and continued roaming about until he found himself again in the middle of the most forlorn wilderness. There he saw the rock – and blood was streaming out of the stone! He saw the dried up spear shaft – and the old hard wood had broken into leaves! He ran to the hut of the wise old man and told him what he had seen.

'Your sins have been forgiven you,' the old man said. 'Now you will never burn in hell. You did a good deed when you rescued that woman. Return to your village, and live once again among men.'

This is the story of the youth and his mother and what they did. The mother of the boy was an evil woman. This is what happens if one always does just what comes into one's mind.

The Unfaithful Wife

A MARRIED woman, whose husband was impotent, fell in love with the Yerima, the son of the Lami'do. Her husband got to know about it. One day, he went out and gathered some poisonous herbs, crushed them together, and made them into a bundle. Then he gathered some medicinal herbs which he also crushed and made up into another bundle. Later, in front of his wife, he opened both bundles, took out some of the medicinal herbs and sprinkled them over his food, which he ate. He then said goodbye to his wife and went off on a trading tour, leaving the deadly poisonous bundle behind in his hut.

As soon as the husband had gone, his wife began to cook maize dumplings and sent for the Yerima. When he came, she put the dumplings and the herbs in front of him and said:

'My husband's herbs give great strength; he put some on his food before he ate.'

The Lami'do's son put a little of the herbs on his dumplings and began to eat. Immediately he drooped, foamed at the mouth and, with the spittle dripping from his lips, died.

Left in the hut all by herself, the woman, now terrified and horror-stricken, cried until midnight, when her gaze suddenly fell on her large hipcloth. She quickly knotted it round her dead lover and went to the wife of a man who was a thief, carrying this bundle on her back.

The thief's wife was fast asleep in her hut, and the doorway was closed with matting. The woman with the bundle on her back knocked and softly called:

'You there, get up and take this.'

Quite drowsy, the thief's wife got up, thinking it was her husband. The woman thrust the bundle containing the corpse through the doorway and returned to her sarē.

A little later, the thief came home and rousing his wife, gave her his bundle, saying: 'You there, take this.'

'Where did you get a second bundle from?' demanded his puzzled wife.

'Is there another bundle?'

'That one over there. Isn't that your bundle?'

'That? I didn't bring it,' exclaimed the astonished man.

'Let's have a look at it,' said his wife.

They dragged the bundle to the middle of the hut, blew on the fire and, opening the bundle, saw the body of the Yerima.

'Allah alone can handle this affair,' the man said, his heart beating violently with fear.

He went outside and looked around. There was not a living soul to be seen; the glimmering fire of the honey-gatherer, who empties the nests of the wild bees at night, was all he could see.

Returning to his hut, he tied up the dead man in a bundle and, putting it on his back, set out for the honey-gatherer. The man was high up in the tree when he arrived.

'Honey-gatherer,' he called out, 'give me some honey.'

'You can't have any right away. I haven't quite finished yet,' the other man replied.

'I shall die if you don't give me some immediately,' said the thief, leaning the corpse against the tree, and he went back to his hut.

When the honey-gatherer had finished, he began to climb down. As he neared the ground, he said to the figure below: 'Careful! I am coming.'

Dead silence! The figure did not move. With his foot he pushed the corpse aside and came down and blew the fire up. Then he saw the Yerima.

'So that's it! Because of the honey you pretend you've died. Well, there's your honey.' He emptied the honey-pot all over the head of the dead man and went home.

The next morning the woodcutters came along and found the dead man. He was completely covered with bees and honey. They spread the news that they had found the Lami'do's son, and that while he was trying to get some honey the bees had killed him.

Ashee! The people didn't know that his mistress had really killed him, and that they had belittled the shrewd-ness of her impotent husband.

The Judge's Jealous Wife

IN HIS sarē, a judge lived with his four wives. One of them, the one he had married first, who was called the Great Woman, or the mother of the household, loved him more than any of the younger ones. But she was a very jealous woman.

Once, on the day when it was her turn to have the judge, her husband, for the night in her hut, she told her little korgel, or servant girl:

'Go to the brook, catch some tiny little fishes and bring them back to me.'

The korgel did as she was told and caught the tiddlers for the Great Woman, who then took a pumpkin, cut it in half and, putting the fishes inside, closed it again. Then she hid the pumpkin next to her hut.

The judge spent the night with her, the Great Woman. Just before dawn he said it was time to get up and go to prayers. Quickly the mother of the household went outside the hut. When the judge came out, there she was with the open pumpkin in her hand and the tiddlers leaping madly about in it. The sight of this made the judge forget prayers and all. As fast as he could he ran to the sarē of the ruler, calling to the man at the gate: 'Tell the Lami'do I must see him at once.'

When he came out, the judge said: 'I saw a pumpkin with tiddlers jumping about inside – I have never seen such a thing in all my life.'

'Come, come, my friend,' replied the Lami'do. 'Can't you think of a better one?'

Just then, the judge's wife, the mother of the household, who had followed her husband, cried:

'The judge is beset by an evil spirit! He was awake all night and didn't sleep a wink. Catch him and put him in irons. He'll start raving any moment.'

'Yes, yes, that's true,' said the Lami'do. 'Just now, before prayers, he insisted on seeing me, and came out with a whopping great lie.'

The people caught the judge and put him in irons.

After two months and ten days, the younger wives got tired of waiting for the judge's return and they left his sarē for good. Immediately, the eldest wife, the Great Woman, went to the Lami'do and begged him:

'Please let my husband come home.'

He was freed. When he returned home, there was only his eldest wife left. Ever afterwards, she kept her husband for herself alone. Such was the trick the Great Woman played to get rid of the younger wives. The judge never married any more, and remained a one-woman man for the rest of his life.

The Two Brothers

THERE WERE once two brothers. The younger possessed everything – thousands upon thousands of camels, thousands and thousands of sheep and thousands and thousands of goats. He owned the whole world, but he only gave the crumbs from his table to his brother. This hurt the elder brother deeply, for he had studied much at school. He was a Malum, a scholar, who had studied all the twelve sciences.

'Poverty is very distressing,' said the elder brother one day. 'I shall go to the Master of the World, who owns everything.'

When he went away he said to his wife: 'I am going away. Farewell, until I return.'

For five hundred years he walked; then he met an old man who lived quite alone in the bush.

'Salamu Aleikum!' he greeted him.

'Aleika Salamu!' replied the old man.

The elder brother stayed with him, and sitting down together they told each other their stories.

In the old man's house there were two calabashes of food. The old man hid one and they ate out of the other. The maize porridge had not come to an end when their hunger was satisfied. The Malum, the elder brother, got up to go.

'If you go to the Master of the World,' the old man said, 'ask him for me where my place is in paradise, because I have done good works for twenty years.'

The Malum replied: 'So be it'. He saluted the old man and went his way.

Later he met a robber in the bush. The robber's sarē stood quite alone in the middle of the bush, and there was no other place in sight. The Malum called at the entrance hut and went in, but only found the robber's wife. She brought him water, and he sat down and drank.

When the robber returned and saw him he said:

'Welcome, friend! You are alone. Where are you going to?'

'I am on my way to the Master of the World,' replied the Malum.

'When you arrive there,' said the robber, 'ask him for me if my place in Hell matches my sins, for I've killed many people. I keep their teeth, piled high in the granary.'

'So be it,' answered the elder brother. 'Now I shall go.'

He saluted him, and left. He travelled to the end of the world. There he found nothing but pitch black darkness. Into this darkness he went, and there he met some angels.

'Where are you going to?' they said.

'Poverty is very distressing. I am on my way to the Master of the World,' he replied.

'Come! We will show you your dwelling in Paradise,' they said. They went with him out of the darkness and showed him his place.

'Praised be the Prophet! Thank God!' said the elder brother.

Then they went back into the darkness with him, and he told them the story of the old man.

'There is no place whatever in Paradise for him, miser that he is. In fire he shall dwell,' they told him.

The Malum then told them the story of the robber. 'Go and tell the robber,' they said, 'that God has forgiven him. He shall dwell in Paradise.'

On his way home he met the robber and said to him: 'Allah has forgiven you all that you have done.'

'Thank God,' he replied. 'I repent of my sins. I abandon robbery. Let us go to a Mosque that I may pray and fast.' And so he accompanied the Malum on his way.

R-B

They met the old man, and told him:

'God has not forgiven you at all. You shall dwell in Hell. You will receive nothing on the judgement day, child of fire that you are.' Then, saluting him, they went back to the Malum's sarē.

The Master of the World turned the elder brother into a rich man and gave him all the things he wanted. Allah gave him the wealth of the whole world and exalted him. He surpassed his younger brother and all the people followed him, the beloved of Allah.

The Three Alims

ALIM, THE flatterer, Alim, the thief, and Alim, the kola nut trader, lived in three quite different villages, but one day they met at a crossroad and began to question each other. Alim, the thief, said:

'I am going to the wife of the Lami'do.'

The other two replied that they too had it in mind to go to the wife of the ruler. Alim, the trader, then suggested: 'From now on, let us go together.'

Alim, the flatterer, said: 'I'll see to it that we are well looked after.'

'If you get us a good bed, I'll steal the wife of the Lami'do,' boasted Alim, the thief.

Alim, the trader, capped this with: 'If you steal her, I'll make love to her.'

They went on until they came to the gates of the town. One behind the other, they filed through the town right into the sarē of the Lami'do.

Alim, the flatterer, said: 'We were like blind men, we three, until we heard of your wonderful powers. Now we are here even we begin to see a little.'

'Samaki, find them a comfortable place to sleep in,' said the ruler turning to his servant. Samaki took them to one of the best resthouses in the town.

After dark, Alim, the thief, went to the back of the Lami'do's sarē, made a hole in the mud wall and, climbing through it, tiptoed to the hut of the wife of the Lami'do. She suddenly saw him and her heart began to beat violently.

'Nobody is allowed here,' she said. Then, gaining confidence, she added: 'What do you want?'

'I've heard about you. It's you I want,' he whispered. 'Gather your clothes together and all the things you like to have round you, and the favourite horse of the Lami'do as well.'

The woman hastily tied her clothes round her, ran and fetched the saddle and put it on the favourite horse of her husband.

'And where is the spear of the Lami'do?' asked Alim, the thief.

The woman went so far as to creep into the Lami'do's hut to fetch the spear for him. Then, with Alim leading the horse in front, they all climbed through the hole in the wall, which he closed again with mud so that it looked as if nothing had happened.

They joined the other two in the resthouse and lay down until cockcrow, when Alim, the thief, said to the others: 'Let us get away from here.'

But Alim, the trader, replied: 'You two are thieves. I am not. I will stay.'

The two others got up and ran away, leaving the woman behind, for by now they were scared stiff.

Alim, the trader, did not stir until the sun was up and the courtiers had gathered in the courtyard of the Lami'do. Then he jumped on the horse, pulled the wife of the Lami'do up behind him, tying her to himself, and rode straight up to the ruler.

The Lami'do opened his eyes very wide indeed, for there he saw a woman, his wife, a horse, his favourite horse, and a spear, his very own spear. Gathering himself together, he beat on the big bell. The courtiers hastily assembled as if there were a threat of war. They tried to catch Alim, the trader, but he knocked two or three of them down and made a gap round the Lami'do, whose own spear was now turned on him. Alim beat the Lami'do on the head until the blood began to flow. At last, he left off and galloped away with the woman still tied on behind, for by now everyone was terrified of him.

Alim, the trader, met the other two, who had waited for him on the road. He lowered the woman to the ground and asked:

'Which of us would you like?'

'Alim, the flatterer,' she replied, and walked away with him. She remained with him three years; then she got tired of him and left him.

Walking along the road, she met Alim, the thief, and lived with him for two years. Then she walked out on him and quickly found Alim, the trader, with whom she stayed for ever and ever.

Two Old Friends

HERE IS a story of a bearded old man and his boyhood friend and neighbour.

One day the old man, who had nine children, said to his friend:

'I have nine children, but only one single slave. When I die you shall split the slave equally among my children. Please do exactly as I have told you.'

'I promise,' pledged his old friend.

Soon after that the old man died. His friend mused: one single slave, nine children? It is better to sell the slave, trade with the money and buy nine slaves.

One day, he took the slave and went on a trading tour. They went this way and that, from one market to another. Wherever they remained for a whole day he offered the slave for sale, but nobody bought him.

Further and further away from their village they walked, passing many towns in their wanderings. Once they arrived at a town seething with news. Here they put up in the sarē of a judge. The old man had to wait until after nightfall before he heard the judge's news.

'Tomorrow they are going to kill me,' the judge said.

'Why are they going to kill you?' asked the bearded old man.

'Our Lami'do is very wicked,' said the judge, adding: 'He has already killed twenty-seven judges and tomorrow is my turn.'

'But why is he going to kill you?' persisted the old man.

'The Lami'do asks: "What are the works of Allah?" That is why he killed all those judges. He cuts off their heads, because there is no one who knows the works of Allah,' the judge moaned.

'Allah protect you!' replied the old man. He went into his hut and lay down until daybreak, when he and the slave got up, said goodbye to the judge and went their way.

While they were walking along, the slave suddenly exclaimed: 'Father, listen! I know the works of Allah.'

'Really, slave? Do you really know them?' asked the astonished old man.

'Yes, I do,' was the slave's reply.

'Let's go back to the judge,' said the old man.

They found the judge in tears.

'Be quiet, don't cry. The Lami'do won't kill you,' said the slave soothingly. 'Go to the place where the prayers are held. When they have finished, go to the ruler and salute him. If he asks you what are the works of Allah, tell him: The works of Allah are very many and varied. He destroys certain people and their realms; others He permits to go on existing. Some become rich; others poor. While some get leprosy, others become blind, lame and ill. Some He appoints to rule, to preach, to beat the drum, while others do absolutely nothing. Some live forever in the bush like evil spirits; some are mad; some are clever; some have a lot of patience; and there are also the fishermen and hunters. Such are the works of Allah. If you tell all that to the Lami'do, he won't kill you.'

The judge did as he was told. He went to the place of prayer and prayed with the others, then followed them up to the ruler and saluted him. The Lami'do questioned him about the works of Allah, and the judge told him what the slave had told him to say about the works of Allah.

'Who on earth told you that?' exclaimed the Lami'do.

'A strange slave with a strange man came and stayed in my sarē. They told me,' replied the judge.

'Go, fetch those two men,' commanded the ruler, who had decided not to kill him.

The judge called the old man and the slave. The Lami'do said: 'Sell me that slave.'

'What will you pay for him?' replied the old man.

'I will pay all the treasures in the world,' the ruler said to the old man.

The old man replied: 'Take him.'

The Lami'do gave the old man untold riches, deprived the judge of his office and appointed the slave in his place because he was so clever.

The bearded old man returned to his sarē and gave all the wealth he brought with him to the children of his old boyhood friend. He kept the promise he had made to the dead man. He took nothing for himself and the children became very rich. That is the truth.

The Jealous Husband

THERE WAS once a man who vowed that he would never marry a gay and light-hearted flirt, only a simple and innocent girl. Some time afterwards, his best friend's wife gave birth to a little girl. On the day her parents named her, he took her to his sarē and handed her over to one of his servants, ordering that the girl must be brought up without knowing anything about the world outside.

When she was old enough, the man went to her father, his best friend, to arrange the marriage. From then on she lived at her husband's sarē for ten years without setting foot outside it, and the only males she saw were the three sons she bore him.

One day, the cunning matchmaker, the pul-woman, chose this guileless young woman to further her plans. She went to her with twenty kola nuts.

'Mother, who sends these kola nuts?' the young woman asked.

The old matchmaker replied: 'You silly little fool, locked up in this sarē. You know nothing about the world outside. There is a marvellous young man; there is nobody like him in the world. It is he who sends you these kola nuts.'

The young woman accepted the kola nuts and gave back ten of them to the old pul-woman, who quickly went up to the first young man she met and said:

'A certain woman sends you greetings. Look at these kola nuts. I've been told to give them to you.'

The puzzled young man exclaimed: 'I haven't even seen her. How does she know me?'

'When you passed at the back of the sarē, she peeped

through the matting of the fence and saw you,' the old pul-woman lied.

'When shall I see her?' asked the young man eagerly.

'As soon as I take you to her,' replied the sly old matchmaker. She went straight back to the guileless young woman, but only to tell her how to escape from her husband's home.

In the early afternoon the young woman began to tremble and shiver. She trembled and trembled and held her breath, so that she seemed to have died. Her husband wept and called the people together. Fearing some dangerous disease, they hastily buried her in the cemetery outside the village.

After sunset, the old pul-woman went to the young man and told him where the young woman was buried. She told him to take some clothes and bangles with him. Quickly he went to the burial ground, dug her out and dressed her in all this finery. So they went away to another country. In this way did the guileless young woman escape from her jealous husband.

The husband wept and said:

'My wife is dead. I shall never marry again. I shall go on a pilgrimage.'

He gathered his things together, taking his three sons with him to beg for food in the towns and villages.

One day they arrived at the town where the wife now lived. The father stayed at the resthouse and sent his sons into the town to beg. Going from sarē to sarē, the children arrived at the home of their mother. It was the mother herself who came to the entrance and gave them food.

The children looked at her and recognized her as their mother. Their mother recognized them, too, as her sons; but neither spoke a word.

When the children returned to their father, the second son said:

'Father, we saw our mother.'

Crying out aloud and weeping, the father moaned:
'The dead never return.'

But the children insisted that they had seen their
mother. The father did not believe them, but the children
would not leave him in peace.

The eldest son said: 'Father, let us go together. Then
you will see her with your own eyes.'

The father agreed to go to the sarē with his sons, and
hid himself near the entrance. The children begged for
food, and once again their mother came out, bringing
them food and presents.

The father, watching from his hideout, saw that it was
really his wife, the mother of his children. He did not
move or say anything at all. But on returning to the
resthouse he spread it all over the town that he had seen
the mother of his sons at a certain place.

The judge heard about it. Calling the court together,
he sent for the woman. When she came, he asked
her:

'Woman, do you know this man?'

She replied that she did not know him.

Turning to the man he said: 'Do you know this
woman?'

'As truly as I touch this Koran, this woman is my wife,'
he replied.

Then the judge spoke: 'Those children over there, do
you know them?'

'No,' answered the woman. 'I do not know them.'

For twenty-five days they held the court, and all this
time the woman insisted that she knew neither the man
nor his children.

One evening, the judge said to his wife: 'This case
about the woman and the man with the three sons is
beyond me.'

'Will you forgive me if I dare to tell you something

about it?' asked his wife, who, as a good daughter of the Prophet, never forgot her place.

'I will forgive you,' the judge replied, and she gave him sound advice.

The next day the court met again. The judge, who had a ram hidden in the hut nearby, said to the woman: 'You have said you did not know these children. All right, I shall kill them.'

'Guard, take the eldest son and kill him,' he commanded.

The guard dragged the eldest son to the hut, where he killed the ram. With his knife dripping with blood, he returned to the court. Then he took the second son away, dipped his knife in the gore of the ram and, with the blood streaming off the blade, went back to fetch the third, the youngest.

'Oh, leave me my little one, my youngest,' the mother begged, beginning to weep aloud.

Then said the judge:

'Do you still say you don't know these children?'

This was how the judge returned the woman to her husband, the father of her children.

Omaru and Wulam Jerre

OMARU! THERE was nobody like him in the whole world: he had such a beautiful body.

'I have more power over women than you,' his friend, Wulam Jerre, boasted one day.

'That's a lie,' replied Omaru. 'There is nobody more powerful than I am.'

Then he added: 'Let us go travelling; we shall see who is the better man.'

'Omaru,' retorted Wulam Jerre, 'a priest has given me the Layaru amulet; no woman in the world can resist me.'

'All right. Let's find out,' Omaru said.

They walked far away to another town. Just outside the walls, they met slaves carrying water into the town. Omaru and Wulam Jerre asked for news of the place. 'Great news,' said the slaves. 'The only daughter of the Lami'do has given birth to a little girl. The water we are carrying is for the young mother's bath.'

'Wulam Jerre,' challenged Omaru, the beautiful, 'send her a message to come today.'

Wulam Jerre sent his message by the slaves, but the reply was: 'It is impossible for me to come. I am still too weak; wait until I am up again.'

Omaru teased Wulam Jerre, saying: 'You won't get her.'

In the same town there was a woman against whom even the gossips had nothing to say. Wulam Jerre sent a message to her as soon as he heard of this. But she replied that she was busy and was in any case not in the habit of receiving strange men.

Omaru, the beautiful, laughed aloud: 'Ha, ha, ha! Hi, ti ti! I can do better than that.'

'Very well,' Wulam Jerre retorted. 'You send to the women. Then we shall see.'

Omaru sent for the daughter of the Lami'do. At once she came, walking openly through the main gates where her father's men were praying; still weak from her confinement, she stumbled past them. In this state she came to Omaru, the beautiful.

Turning to Wulam Jerre, he sang:

> 'I can do more than you.
> I need only snap my fingers;
> Immediately she winks at me.
> I sit down and she sits down;
> I talk and she talks.
>
> I bring her kola nuts,
> And we eat them together.
> I say to her "See you again,"
> And off she goes, back to her hut.'

Soon afterwards, Omaru sent for the other woman, the one whose life was beyond reproach. Naked but for her white beads round her hips, she came to him at once and sat down with him on the same mat.

Looking at Wulam Jerre, he taunted him: 'Wulam Jerre, I am more powerful than you.'

He began to sing:

> 'You man there, the night is your enemy;
> You man there, you have to sleep alone.
> The woman is great, but you are her child.'

Wulam Jerre buried his head in his hands and, crying bitterly, said: 'It is true, Omaru, you are by far the more powerful. Ashee! I had no cause to be so conceited.'

The Piebald Stallion

A FATHER died and left his son a stallion, a piebald with black knees. This horse was proud, courageous of heart, fast as the wind and a great jumper.

One day, the young man began to saddle his stallion. First, he put on it a richly ornamented saddle-cloth, then saddle-bags with finely embroidered cushions, and a headpiece with silver ornaments. Next, he went to his best friend and said: 'I've heard people talking about the beauty of the wife of a certain Lami'do. As true as I stand before you, I am about to ride there now to fetch her.'

Mounting his horse, he rode throughout the whole day till nightfall. He did the same the next day and, on the evening of the third day, he reached the town where the woman of his choice lived.

He dismounted at the sarē of the old pul-woman, the matchmaker, and slept there in a little grass hut next to his horse. In the morning, he called for the old matchmaker, the pul-woman. She came, they greeted each other, and after they had exchanged news he came to the point:

'Mother,' he murmured, 'what brought me here is the people's talk about the beauty of the Lami'do's most beloved wife. I have fallen in love with her. I do indeed love her!'

'The Governor of our town is a wicked man, my child,' she warned him. 'His heart is as black as a thunder cloud.'

The young man took a beautiful cloth and gave it to the matchmaker, the pul-woman. She thought for a bit, scratched her head and then said: 'So be it. Thank you. Allah bless you.'

'Now go to this woman,' said the youth, 'and let her know that I shall be coming.'

The pul-woman took her little broken begging bowl and stick and limped into the sarē of the Lami'do. The Governor and his followers were sitting outside in the first courtyard. The old matchmaker tried to slip past them, but the guards stopped her. But the Lami'do said: 'Let her pass;' so on she went. In the sarē itself, she doubled up, pressed her hand against her belly as though in great pain and lurched into the hut of the most beloved wife of the Lami'do.

The wife bade her welcome and, after they had exchanged greetings, the pul-woman said: 'I have seen something I have never seen in all my life before.'

'What was that?' the wife asked.

The old matchmaker replied: 'A young man has arrived in this town. He has a tiny little beard and all the beauty a man could possibly wish for. He came yesterday in the cool of the evening on his stallion, a beautiful piebald with black knees, and as fast as an arrow. His owner sends me to tell you that he loves you.'

All this did the old matchmaker say, but the wife replied:

'You know the Lami'do is terribly jealous, though there is no reason for it; I sleep with no one but him. He has fifty-eight wives, but visits none of them. He only comes to me. Every night he is in my hut.'

'If you tell the young man to come, he will come,' answered the old matchmaker.

'But if the Lami'do sees him in the sarē, he'll kill him,' she exclaimed.

'This youth,' said the old pul-woman, 'does not know what fear means.'

'Then tell him to come,' the wife replied.

The old matchmaker returned to her sarē and told the young man everything that had passed between her and the most beloved wife of the Lami'do. Next morning, before dawn, she said to him: 'I wonder if you dare go to her?'

The reply of the young man was to saddle his stallion and tie him in the sarē. Then he took the old pul-woman's clothes and put them on, smeared ashes over his face and arms, took the little broken bowl and stick and limped into the sarē of the ruler.

It was still very early, and the Lami'do and his courtiers were sitting in the entrance hut. The youth, looking exactly like the old pul-woman, passed them without any interference and entered the hut of the most beloved wife of the Lami'do. They talked to each other and very quickly agreed to run away together. She gathered up her bangles and beads, taking everything that belonged to her, and the two of them climbed to the top of the mud wall at the back of the sarē, jumped down and so got away.

They ran to the old matchmaker. Here, putting on his own clothes again, the young man said to her:

'I've taken the wife of the Lami'do, his best beloved, and I shall ride away with her past the entrance hut and past the eyes of the ruler!'

'Well done, well done!' shouted the old pul-woman.

The young man mounted his piebald stallion, put the wife of the Lami'do in front of him, and rode up to the entrance hut. The Lami'do looked at the youth, looked at the horse and looked at the woman. His courtiers and servants sat in dead silence whilst they saw the young man approach, stop his horse, and say to the Lami'do:

'I've taken your wife from you. I am now riding away with her. We shall marry.'

At last it dawned on the ruler that it was his most beloved wife that was sitting on the piebald stallion with the black knees! He raged with fury; his curses sounded like the thunder in a storm. The young man gently spurred his horse and off they went, quicker than lightning.

The Lami'do and his courtiers ran to their horses and gave chase.

The piebald stallion with the black knees galloped faster than the wind. They came to a broad river. The youth gave a touch of the spurs, and the horse leaped right across the rushing torrent of water. On the other side, he dismounted on the white sand, and lifted down his woman, the best beloved. She took off all her clothes, and with only the white stringed beads round her thighs she went into the water to bathe.

By now the Lami'do and his followers had arrived on the opposite bank of the river. Far away, on the other side of the water, he saw his own best beloved wife, naked, bathing in the river! Yelling and cursing, he ordered his men to fetch her back at once. They rode into the swiftly moving river, full of rapids, three hundred and three men with their horses. They all went into the river, and they were all drowned.

At last, the oldest adviser of the Lami'do turned to him and said: 'Let it be. You've drowned all your servants for the sake of a woman.'

Reluctantly, the Lami'do mounted his horse and with the rest of his followers returned to town.

The young man mounted his stallion and with his woman, the best beloved, rode home. They married and lived happily ever after. And all this was only possible because a piebald stallion with black knees is the finest horse in the world. He is stronger and more courageous than any other horse. So it happened that the young man eloped with the most beloved wife of the Lami'do.

Samandakare

'IT WAS pitch dark last night. Was it dark at your place too?' asked the Lami'do.

Samandakare, who had been summoned to his side, replied: 'Allah bless you, Lami'do. There was even darkness in the beard of my grandfather, so that his moustache walked off and sat itself in the place where his whiskers ought to be.'

'Where is your mother?' was the next question of the Lami'do.

'My mother wanted to dress her hair, but as she forgot her head, she had to go back to fetch it,' Samandakare informed him.

After a pause of some length, the Lami'do ventured: 'Where is your father?'

'Blessings on you, Lami'do! Where my father is, the road has been torn apart, and he went out to knot it together.'

The Lami'do did not attempt to ask any more questions, and Samandakare went home.

Later on, the Lami'do gave an order that the heads of his two slave children should be shaved. Then he told the children: 'Go to Samandakare and tell him that he may dress your hair.'

They found only his father and mother at home when they arrived, for Samandakare had just gone out.

'The Lami'do has sent us,' they said, 'so that Samandakare shall dress our hair.'

The mother and father of Samandakare both wept, and cried: 'Their heads are shaved! How can they be dressed?'

When he returned, Samandakare demanded: 'What are you crying about?'

'The Lami'do has ordered you to dress the hair of his two slave children, but they haven't a single hair on their heads. He has shaved them so close, they are quite bald! That's why we are crying!' they exclaimed.

'Stop crying!' Samandakare said. Taking two little bottle gourds, he filled them with water and gave them to the two children, saying: 'Churn this until butter comes; then I shall dress your hair.'

They churned and churned, but no butter formed in the gourds. At sunset the children gave up and went back to the Lami'do, who asked them:

'Why didn't Samandakare dress your hair?'

'He gave us water,' they replied, 'and told us to churn it. He said that as soon as butter formed, he would dress our hair.'

The next morning, the Lami'do sent for Samandakare.

'How is it possible to churn water into butter?' he demanded.

'How is it possible to dress the hair of heads that are shaved clean?' retorted Samandakare.

'There is my bull,' the Lami'do said. 'Make him pregnant, so that he calves today; milk him; then churn the milk into butter and bring it to me, so that I can make medicine with it this very day,' he ordered.

Samandakare went away and fetched some pumpkin seeds. Giving them to the Lami'do, he said: 'Take these pumpkin seeds. See that they sprout and grow today; cut the pumpkin and divide it in half; then clean it out thoroughly and give me the bowls to receive the milk.'

'But how can I do all that in one day?' asked the slow-witted Lami'do.

'Ihi! ihi!' sniggered Samandakare. 'And how shall the bull calve today? If he does, I shall milk him and bring the bull-milk to you at once.'

'This is a seed of cotton,' countered the Lami'do. 'Sow it today; make it grow leaves, flower and bear fruit; then make the fruit ripen and burst. Gather the cotton, spin it, weave it and sew it together into a fine robe for me, all this very day.'

'Take these seeds of the great calabash pumpkin,' Samandakare retorted. 'Go and plant it today. Make it grow and bear a large pumpkin. Split it in half; clean it out properly and bring me the bowls, so that I can use them as a casket when I present you with the fine robe.'

'But, Samandakare, how shall I do all that in one day?' protested the Lami'do impatiently.

'If you cannot do it,' replied Samandakare tartly, 'then I shan't plant, harvest, spin and weave the cotton, nor sew you a great robe today.'

All this was too much for the Lami'do; he made up his mind to kill Samandakare. He ordered a strong hut with a stout door to be built. Samandakare was caught and thrown into it, but he had some old bones in his pocket. Later on, the children came out and walked round the hut. They heard him crunching at something and inquired: 'Samandakare, what are you gnawing?'

'Your father has hidden me because I was eating something very sweet – the sweetest food in the world,' he said. Then he added: 'If you would like some of it, you must let me out, so that I can give you a tiny little bit – only a tiny little bit, mark you!'

The children opened the door. Samandakare came out and caught the children. Pushing them gently into the hut, he barred the door and walked away.

At sunset, the time of the evening prayer, when no one was about, the Lami'do ordered the hut to be burnt down. As the flames grew hot, the children inside screamed: 'Father, it is us, your children, inside!'

But the Lami'do only replied: 'I did not beget you.'

The hut was completely gutted, and the children were

burnt to death, for the Lami'do did not know that he had killed his own children. Later, whom did he see approaching but Samandakare. When Samandakare came nearer, he sat down and saluted the Lami'do. The Lami'do refused to acknowledge the greeting.

Then Samandakare baited him: 'How clever, to burn your own children to death!'

The ruler ordered him to be seized and put in chains, but just before they fettered him in a dark corner of the sarē, Samandakare stole the little silver stool of the Lami'do's wife, and hid it in his robes.

Some time later, the Lami'do, his wife and his courtiers went outside the town to hold court. When they sat down, his wife missed her little silver stool and asked leave to fetch it. Two guards were ordered to go with her. When they came to the sarē, the men remained in the entrance hut and the woman went on alone to search for her stool. She searched everywhere, but could not find it until she came upon Samandakare chained up in a dark corner.

'Have you seen my little stool?' she asked.

'If you want it,' he replied, 'you must set me free.'

The woman loosened the chains, whereupon Samandakare seized her and quickly stripped her of her clothes. He pulled off her bead girdle and put it on himself, tore off her bangles and slipped them on his arms, arranged her headcloth over his face and, putting the little silver stool on his head, rejoined the guards in the entrance hut. Looking exactly like the Lami'do's wife, he walked on in front of the men and all three returned to the court.

At the time of the great prayer, the Lami'do, his supposed wife, and everybody else returned to the sarē. A slave girl heated some hot water for a bath for Samandakare, whom everybody believed to be the Lami'do's wife. He bathed himself, went into the hut of the Lami'do and lay down on the bed. There he stayed quietly until late at night, when the Lami'do came in. The two of them whispered together for a long time in the darkness until the ruler fell asleep.

An ancient battle-sword hung on the wall beside the bed. Samandakare took it and cut off the Lami'do's head, dragged him out of the hut and threw his body outside the sarē. Then he struck the great bell; the people gathered together and proclaimed Samandakare as Lami'do.

The Old Pul-Woman and the Devil

ONE DAY, at the end of Ramadan, the old pul-woman took her little gourd and went to market. On the way she met Shedan, the devil.

'Come with me,' he said. 'I will show you how I can cause destruction.'

The woman followed him. When they arrived at the market, the devil whispered:

'Sit over there and watch. I will show you what I can do.'

'All right,' replied the old pul-woman.

Some negroes, pagans from Bamle, who because of their unbelief were not very welcome during this festival, were just coming into the market. Many of them had their dogs with them. The devil stood near the place in the market where the butchers had squatted together and were cutting choice fat meat into long strips. He made the dogs run up to the bench on which the meat lay, to steal some of it. A butcher saw one of the dogs and stabbed it with a knife.

'Did you stab my dog?' the owner demanded.

'Yes, I did,' retorted the butcher.

The pagan took his bow and hit him over the head. The hearts of all the butchers became black with fury at this deed done by an unbeliever. They jumped up to fight the pagans, and a bloody battle took place. Many of the pagans were killed and the pagans left many of the butchers dead. In the end, the market was quite empty. The booths were all smashed up, and there were no people to be seen.

'Did you see what I have done?' asked the devil

proudly as he went over and spoke to the old pul-woman.

'Yes' she answered. 'But I can do better.'

'All right! Try! But I want to see it with my own eyes,' challenged the devil.

'Come here tomorrow morning,' she replied, 'and you shall see me at work.'

'Agreed,' said the devil.

The old pul-woman returned to her sarē, put down her little gourd and went to the home of the ruler. The courtiers were assembled in the large entrance hut, and when they saw her coming they wanted to stop her, but the Lami'do said: 'No, let her come in; she can get something to eat in the sarē.'

The old woman walked on and went straight to the hut of the favourite wife of the Lami'do. Here she salaamed, then entered in. Immediately after they had greeted each other, the old pul-woman said: 'Someone, the son of a certain man, sends me to you – such and such is the position.'

'But how can I see him? I am not allowed out of the sarē,' replied the favourite wife of the ruler.

'Hi! hi!' answered the old woman. 'That is not difficult.'

The wife then agreed to the proposal, and the pul-woman said: 'Now I am going home.'

The wife made her a present of a wonderful, long piece of fat, some high meat and cornflour.

Later in the day, the old pul-woman went to the sarē of the Waziri. He was a very wealthy man but had only one child, a son. She called to the youth through the fence and he came out to her. Quickly she repeated the same story, but this time about a woman.

'But I don't know her, and she doesn't know me. I am scared,' the youth exclaimed.

'You don't need to be,' said the old woman soothingly.

'All right; I'd like to see her.'

'Tomorrow morning, before sunrise, you must come

to my hut,' the pul-woman directed. The youth agreed.

Before sunrise, the young man got up and went to the old woman.

'Come along, I'll put you into the big water pot,' she told him.

He got into the pot, and she covered it up and rolled it into the sarē of the Lami'do. There she met all the men on horseback ready to ride outside the town for the prayer. She rolled the water pot past them into the sarē, right on until she was in front of the hut of the ruler's favourite wife. She rolled it up to the doorway.

'Here, take this!' she said.

The woman took the pot inside, and when she opened it there she saw the young man. He crawled out of the pot and the two sat down and chatted together.

In the meanwhile, the old pul-woman went to the Lami'do and told him:

'I saw the son of the Waziri in the hut of your favourite wife.'

Immediately, everyone jumped off his horse, ran back into the sarē followed by the Lami'do, and found the youth. They killed him. The Lami'do was so furious that he even refused to ride out afterwards to the prayer.

The old pul-woman now went to the sarē of the Waziri.

'The Lami'do has killed your son,' she told him.

The Waziri's heart was sorely stricken. 'My child! My only son! The Lami'do has killed him!'

'Hi! hi!' sniggered the old woman. 'He killed him.'

The Waziri summoned his clan to wage war on the Lami'do. They rode to the sarē of the ruler and fought. Many were killed before the war was ended.

'Shedan, did you see my work?' asked the old pul-woman proudly.

'Yes,' said the devil. 'You can do it much better than I.'

Such were the deeds of the old pul-woman and the devil. The old woman was very wicked.

The Vagabond and the Djinn

THE DJINN had married a dijajo, a shrew. The vagabond, too, had married a dijajo. One day the djinn ran away from his wife.

The vagabond was hungry and had no clothes. One day, he filled his little water gourd and ran away from his dijajo. On the road, he met the djinn, and they sat down for a rest.

'Friend, where do you come from?' asked the djinn.

'I've run away from my wife. She is a dijajo,' replied the vagabond.

'A! A! I too ran away because of my wife, and she too is a dijajo,' said the djinn, adding: 'So we are fellow-sufferers.'

From that day on these two travelled together, until they came to the gates of a town with a very thick and high wall.

Halting outside the gates, the djinn said: 'Listen, my friend: I've got the following plan. The daughter of the Lami'do of this town is going to be married: in fact, they are already making preparations for the wedding. Now, I shall crawl into her head, and, whatever they do, I will not come out until I see you. When I do come out, I want to marry one of her playmates. But as long as they promise you only position and wealth, and not her hand in marriage, don't let me see you. If, in spite of my warning, you dare come within range of my eyes, I shall kill you.' The vagabond agreed, but he was frightened.

They both walked into the town, and the djinn immediately entered into the head of the young bride. She started to behave as though threatened with death, and tore off all her clothes. Her father spent a lot of money trying to cure her, but finally gave up in despair.

The vagabond now came forward and said:

'If I succeed in curing the girl, will you give her to me in marriage?'

'Yes, indeed, I will,' swore her father.

Filling his gourd with water, the vagabond immediately went into the hut of the girl, where she lay in chains.

'Free her!' he commanded. They took off her chains. Then he spat on her and said spells over her whole body. At once the djinn came out, ran outside and possessed one of her playmates. And that's how it happened that the vagabond married the daughter of the Lami'do.

The father of the other girl now came and begged the Lami'do: 'Please make your son-in-law drive the djinn out of the head of my daughter.'

The Lami'do gave his consent, but the vagabond, who by now was very frightened, said: 'I will drive him out, but this time I will do it outside the town.'

They took the girl outside the walls of the town. The vagabond quickly put on his old rags, picked up his little water gourd and went and found the girl. As soon as he was in front of her, he said to the djinn: 'I don't see you. You don't see me. I'm not here.' Then, turning in every direction, he suddenly shouted: 'Isn't that my dijajo and yours coming towards us? They have followed us!'

The djinn, terrified, dashed away as fast as he could. The vagabond sauntered away, leaving his wife and wealth. He wasn't at all sure that the djinn would not return to the town; he just did not trust him.

The Finicky Maiden

ONCE UPON a time there was a young girl who swore that she would only fall in love and marry a man with a perfectly spotless skin. Who he was or where he came from didn't matter, so long as there wasn't a single pimple on his body. She waited a very, very long time for such a man.

At last, the Bushkuunga heard about her. He put on three wonderful robes one over the other; the top robe was richly embroidered. Then, having donned a beautiful pair of trousers, an elegantly tucked cap, a magnificent sword and a pair of finely wrought sandals, he looked exactly like a human being. No sooner had the young girl seen him than she fell in love with him. They talked things over and got married.

A few days after the marriage, her husband said that it was time to go to his home. The young wife took her korgel, her slave girl, and the three of them began a journey far off into the middle of the wilderness.

On the way, the man's sword suddenly dropped on the path. His wife exclaimed: 'But you have lost your sword!'

'Never mind,' said her husband, 'I will find it again.'

'Now you have lost your cap!' she cried when, a little further on, his elegant cap fell on the ground.

'Leave it alone; I'll find it again,' he said a little impatiently.

But again, a little while after this, she had to cry out: 'You've lost your sandals!'

'It doesn't matter,' was the abrupt reply. Then he said:

'If a woman wanted to run away from her husband, where do you think she would hide?'

'Everywhere,' answered his wife. 'She could hide herself everywhere. A woman could hide in the hole in the tree, the cave in the rocks, or in the bushes. ...' So she went on talking of hiding-places, until she was about to say: 'Under cow dung,' but her little korgel whispered: 'Be quiet, stop talking; don't mention cow dung.'

By now the 'man' had lost all his clothes; only a little scarf hung round his neck. Suddenly he jumped into the high grass, rolled himself over and over till he reached the foot of an ant heap, and turned himself back into the Bushkuunga, with the skin of an elephant, a horn on his nose and his whole body covered with hair so long that it dragged along the ground.

The Bushkuunga and the terrified woman went on walking until they came to a Jabi tree with branches hanging down.

'Sit down here in the shade,' the Bushkuunga growled to the woman.

The woman sat down. The Bushkuunga put his head on his wife's lap and ordered: 'Pick the lice off me.'

The young wife picked the lice off him, and the Bushkuunga soon fell asleep. Immediately the two women got up, took the long strands of his hair and tied them round the branches and twigs of the Jabi tree. Then they took all the little bells they had on their ear-rings and bangles and fastened them to the hair of the Bushkuunga. When they had done this, they ran away as fast as they could.

When the Bushkuunga woke up and didn't see his wife, he tried to get up, but fell down because his hair pulled him back. At last he tore himself free and ran after the two women. He searched among the bushes, didn't find them. He looked into the caves; they were not there. He peeped into the holes of the trees, they were empty. Jingle-jangle, jingle-jangle, went his bells through the wilderness; and when the young wife and her korgel heard him coming they lifted a piece of cow dung and crept underneath it.

The Bushkuunga came and planted himself in front of the cow dung and roared: 'Is there anyone underneath this cow dung?' But the cow dung was silent. It didn't move, and the Bushkuunga went away.

Then the women crawled out from underneath the cow dung and went back to their village. Later, the Bushkuunga followed them and turned himself into a Tshabuli tree covered with sweet berries. All the village came to pick the luscious fruit, but the young wife and her korgel did not go near it. They knew it was really the Bushkuunga.

After some time had passed, the young woman met an old and ugly man. She married him and settled down, vowing that she would never leave her village again. That is the story of the finicky young woman and the Bushkuunga.

Babankame and Bankame

THEIR WATER pot was as big as a house.

Babankame said to his son: 'Bankame, get up! Fetch us some water!'

Bankame took the water pot, hung it on his shoulder, went to the river and sank the pot deep into the water. Crocodiles, hippos, big fish, they all entered the pot. When it was quite filled, he hung it on his shoulder and went back to his father.

His father took the pot and drank deeply. Crocodiles, hippos and big fish, they all went down his throat. 'Not even a good mouthful,' he grumbled.

The Lami'do heard about this story. 'I will satisfy their hunger,' he pledged.

He brought his slaves and made them build a shed with poles as thick as a man's body. They made a huge mound of maize porridge and busirije and put it in the shed.

The Lami'do then sent for these two. They came, Babankame and Bankame. They went up to the porridge, the baskets, the pots – all for them alone. They also took into the huge shed the sheep that the Lami'do had brought for them.

Then the people came. They shut them up inside the shed. They blew on the fires to keep Babankame and Bankame warm until early morning, when they woke up.

At once the father Babankame said: 'Bankame, get up! Let's go home. It is cold here, and hunger gnaws my very vitals.'

And so they left the Lami'do. In spite of everything, they were not satisfied.

The Monkey who went Begging

ONE DAY, the monkey wanted to go begging. He asked his neighbours which of them would like to go with him. His neighbours, the dogs, replied: 'The partridge can go if she likes.'

The partridge agreed. The monkey, taking his spoon and knife, handed them to the partridge, saying: 'If we beg for food, the people are sure not to give us a spoon: and here is a knife as well. We won't get one of those either. You had better carry them.' Then they started along the road together.

As they were approaching a village, the monkey told the partridge: 'Hide the knife and spoon; people might steal them.'

The partridge hid them in the grass, and they walked into the village and begged in a sarē. The owner came out and gave them some flour soup.

The monkey turned at once to the partridge: 'Go and get the spoon.'

The partridge walked all the way back and fetched the spoon. Meanwhile, the monkey drank the soup and even licked the last drops of the bowl before he handed it back. At last the partridge returned. The monkey told her that she had been much too slow and that the owner had taken the soup away. 'I didn't have one drop of it,' he moaned.

The man now came out to them with meat.

'Quick! Run and get the knife!' ordered the monkey. The partridge ran as fast as she could, and returned with the knife. But in the meantime the monkey had roasted the meat and eaten it all up, and what was left he threw into the fire.

'You took much too long. The man took the meat away. Believe it or not: it's the truth!' So he chided the partridge when she arrived at last.

Thus did the monkey play a very dirty trick on the partridge. The poor bird felt so miserable and weak, so hungry and so tired, that she wanted to die.

'I want to go home,' she groaned.

The monkey saw a huge thunderstorm with pitch black clouds slowly rising up the sky, but in spite of this he said to the partridge: 'Get up! We'll go home,' and they started off.

When they came near the river, the storm broke and it poured with rain. They both got thoroughly drenched. When the rain was over, the monkey said:

'Let's gather some wood and make a fire.'

They collected the wood, and the monkey made a fire. As they were drying themselves, he asked her: 'Which do you think is worse? Burning in fire or drowning in water?' adding quickly: 'You stay here. I will try the water. If you see it getting red, you'll know that I am dead. Then you jump into the fire!'

With that he dived into the river. But he had taken a piece of red ochre with him which he rubbed in the water until it became as red as fire.

As soon as he heard the screams of the partridge, he waded out of the river, walked over to the fire and slowly turned the partridge round and round until she was well roasted. Then he ate her up and started on his way home.

As soon as he approached his village, he began to cry and wail: 'The partridge is dead! The partridge is dead!'

'There won't be any ill-feeling about it between us. It's the work of Allah,' his neighbours, the dogs, said, to comfort him.

Time passed and the monkey wanted to go begging again. 'The quail wants to go with you,' said the dogs, his neighbours. The monkey fetched his knife and spoon and gave them to the quail to carry. And so they started off together.

When they were near the village the monkey said: 'You had better hide the knife and the spoon.' But the quail did not hide them in the grass. She put them in her armpits, under her wings.

They entered the village and went to the same man. He brought them soup, and the monkey said: 'Go and get the spoon.'

The quail just walked outside the entrance hut, took the spoon from her armpit and returned to catch the monkey swallowing the soup.

'How were you able to come back as quickly as all that?' he shouted. 'There, you can drink it. I don't like it,' he added angrily, pushing the bowl of soup away.

The quail drank her fill of the soup. Then the man brought some meat, and the monkey told the quail to fetch the knife. As quickly as possible, the quail ran outside, took the knife from her armpit and returned to see the monkey eating the meat.

The monkey was very angry indeed when he saw the quail and threw the meat at her, but the quail took it and ate it quietly. It began to dawn on the monkey that the quail was not at all stupid.

Again, a pitch black thunderstorm slowly came nearer and nearer. When the monkey saw it, he said: 'Get up, quail. It's time to go home.'

They began walking. By the time they got to the river the storm had broken and they got thoroughly soaked.

When it was over, the monkey and quail made a fire. Whilst they were drying themselves, the monkey again asked:

'To be burned in the fire or to be drowned in water: which is worse?' Before the quail could reply, he added: 'You stay here. I'll try the water. If you see it getting red you'll know I am dead. Then you jump into the fire!'

He leapt into the river, rubbing his piece of red ochre. The quail saw the water getting red. She took the monkey's sandals and threw them into the fire, but she herself jumped into his big leather bag. As soon as the monkey heard his sandals in the fire making a noise like 'fon-jon-jon', he came out of the water. Thinking the quail was dead, he turned his sandals round and round until they were well done. Taking them out of the smouldering embers, he hung his bag on his shoulders and started for home.

'This quail is as tough as leather,' he remarked, with a mouth full of his sandals. 'The partridge was much tenderer.'

The quail in his bag could not help cheeping: 'Monkey, you are mad! You are eating your own sandals!'

But the monkey thought his bag was squeaking, and sang:

'Bag, are you singing a song?
Yes, you, what does it mean?
Bag, you are singing a song!'

When he reached the village, he again began to cry and wail: 'The quail is dead! The quail is dead!'

But the quail put her head out of the bag and shouted: 'Monkey, you are a liar! You killed and ate the partridge!'

The dogs no sooner heard this than they came out to attack the monkey, but he ran away into the bush. Ever since then, the monkey lives in the bush and the village dogs and the monkeys can't stand each other. Whenever a dog succeeds in catching a monkey he kills him.

Talul, Talul

LONG, LONG ago, a hyena, a goat and a bushrat were travelling together when they met the Kuunga.

The Kuunga is, as you know, as terrible as a thunderstorm. He asked them: 'Where are you going to?'

The hyena and the goat replied: 'We are going to fetch our dowry.'

But the canny bushrat said: 'As far as I am concerned, I am a young scholar.'

'Write me a magic spell nobody else knows,' demanded the terrible Kuunga.

'I haven't anything to write it on,' answered the bushrat. 'But if I do write it down for you, you could become even more terrible and beautiful than you are!'

Eagerly, the Kuunga said: 'Write it on the skin of the hyena.'

'Don't you see that the hyena is behind you? Get a piece of skin from her yourself. She wouldn't like to give it to me,' replied the bushrat, who would not even have dared to ask.

The Kuunga turned to the hyena and said: 'Please give me a little piece of your skin.'

The hyena, who was very frightened, tore a tiny piece of skin off her body. The Kuunga took it and gave it to the bushrat. The bushrat wrote the spell on it; then she dipped it in honey, for she knew that the Kuunga had a sweet tooth, and gave it to him, saying: 'Lick the spell off and return the skin to me: I'll write you another one.' The Kuunga gulped down the spell, skin and all.

'A! A! You've swallowed it! Where shall we get another piece of skin?'

The terrible Kuunga looked questioningly at the hyena, but the hyena ran away as fast as she could, with the Kuunga in hot pursuit. The goat and the bushrat then took to their heels, and so ends the story.

Thanks to the shrewdness of the bushrat, the Kuunga didn't do them any harm.

The Pig-Headed Younger Brother

ONCE UPON a time there was a boy called Omaru, who had an A'da, an elder sister. Their father and mother were very rich. One day the father said to his first-born, the A'da: 'Whatever your younger brother wishes to do in the future, let him do it. Do not forbid him anything. Let him do exactly as he likes with his wealth.' The father and mother died, and the two children were left alone with great riches.

When Omaru was grown up, he began to waste his inheritance quite stupidly. He took slaves and killed them for no reason at all. He caught and slaughtered milch cows just for a whim; and so he went on until there was nothing left of his great wealth. His A'da reproached him, but he reminded her of their father's last wish before he died; so the elder sister said no more.

Some time later, the elder sister said to Omaru: 'Let us go away from here. Let us go out into the world.'

Omaru agreed. By now, only one single slave girl was left out of all his vast possessions, and she was pregnant; but the brother and sister took her with them on their journey.

Walking along one day, Omaru suddenly said:

'A'da, I am going to kill the slave girl. I want to see what's in her belly.'

'Then do so,' answered his elder sister.

Omaru killed the girl, and now they were quite destitute; nothing was left to them.

For a long, long time they walked, until they came to a river. There wasn't a canoe to take them across, so they sat down and waited till one afternoon a buzzard appeared and said to them:

'If somebody did you a good deed, would you return it with a bad one?'

'Buzzard,' replied the brother and sister, 'we wouldn't do you any harm.'

'Come and sit down on my wings.' The two of them sat on his wings, and the buzzard flew high up in the air.

Just as it was above the middle of the river, Omaru shouted: 'A'da, give me your hairpin.'

'What do you want it for?' she asked.

'To prick the buzzard under his tail,' said Omaru.

'But,' cried A'da, 'the buzzard is carrying us across the river. Yet you, you want to prick him under the tail.'

'I will prick him,' yelled Omaru.

'You won't,' retorted his sister, but it was already too late. He had pricked the buzzard. The bird shook them off and let them drop into the middle of the river.

Deep underneath the water was a large village. Omaru and his sister walked in. The people showed them huts where they could spend the night, but told them that after dark no one was allowed outside, because the wild animals from the bush prowled about the village and killed many people. Omaru promised that he would lie down and sleep and not leave his hut. He then made a fire but as soon as it was dark he went outside and lay down in front of his hut, despite his promise.

In the middle of the night, some leopards came loping towards him. Omaru took two arrows out of his quiver, drew his bow and shot and killed one of them. Another roared, and Omaru shot and killed it. A third rushed towards him and he killed this one too. So he went on until he had killed all the leopards.

A huge buffalo suddenly appeared, with lowered horns, ready to charge; he stood in front of Omaru. Quickly, Omaru took out another arrow and shot the buffalo dead.

Then he took a knife and cut off the tails of the dead animals and carried them into his hut.

Next day, when the sun had risen, the people of the village crowded together, asking: 'Who killed all these animals?'

Some said: 'It must have been that youth who came to us yesterday with his sister.'

The Lami'do of the village gave Omaru thirty horses, sixty cows, and many, many other things; and besides this, a large sarē to live in. All these things the ruler gave to Omaru because he killed the wild beasts. This was how Omaru became rich again.

In the end, the Lami'do gave him his only daughter in marriage. Omaru said to his sister: 'Though I wasted away and squandered our inheritance, now we are rich again.'

'You have said it,' was the only reply of his A'da.

Omaru lived with his wife and sister in this large sarē. He had it scrupulously cleaned, and erected many fences of matting. He had the paths covered with milk-white pebbles, and a large hut with two entrances built in the middle of his sarē. As it says in our fairy tales, he built himself a wonderful palace and adorned it with gold and precious stones.

When the Lami'do died, Omaru summoned the assembly of elders, and the bearded old men made him ruler over the village. Thus did Allah confer kingship on the younger brother in this world, and ever since then he rules and will continue to rule for ever and ever.

The Woman and her Child

ONCE UPON a time, a woman and her child went into the wilderness. In the wilderness they built a tiny little hut for themselves. One day, the woman locked the hut and, putting a piece of matting in front of the doorway, went out to dress the bald heads of the guinea fowls. She dressed the head of one, but wrung the neck of the other and hid it in a hole. On the way home, she picked it up and brought it with her. When she arrived at the tiny little hut, she called out to the child:

'Nana, push the matting away!
In the middle of the wilderness the moon shines upon
me,
In the middle of the wilderness the starlight shines upon
me.'

Nana quickly pushed the matting aside, and the mother entered. They plucked the guinea fowl together and ate it. The next day the woman went out again, and this she did many times.

One day, the hyena found the lonely little hut. She went at once to a sorcerer and said: 'Soften my voice,' for she had a very harsh voice.

The sorcerer softened her voice, and the hyena went to the lonely, little hut and called out:

'Nana, push the matting away!
In the middle of the wilderness the moon shines upon
me,
In the middle of the wilderness the starlight shines upon
me.'

Nana pushed the matting aside, for she thought it was her mother. The hyena entered the little hut and ate the child up. Then she ran away, far, far away.

The mother of the child came back and, calling to her Nana, said:

'Nana, push the matting away!
In the middle of the wilderness the moon shines upon
me,
In the middle of the wilderness the starlight shines upon
me.'

But the mother of the child got no reply. There was only silence. When she entered the hut, she saw that the hyena had eaten her child. She cried bitterly. Then she stopped weeping, plucked her guinea fowl, and ate it and gnawed the bones.

Now she lived quite alone in the wilderness, and from that time on this lonely woman sang a song taunting the hyena:

'As far as I am concerned, I eat big fish,
I eat big fish,
I eat big fish.
Rag-tag and bobtail eat little stinkfish,
Rag-tag and bobtail eat dirt;
As far as I am concerned, I eat big fish.'

Or, to put it in another way:

'As far as I am concerned, I eat roast beef,
I eat roast beef.
Filthy hyenas eat corpses,
Filthy hyenas eat dirt;
But I! I eat roast beef.'

The Story of the Mouse

ONE DAY, a very large snake came and crawled about in the village between the sarēs. The people gathered together in a crowd and wanted to kill it; but a young man, whose father had died and left him three slaves, pleaded that it should not be killed. The people told him that they would only leave the snake in peace if he gave them one of his slaves.

'Then leave it alone,' he said, and gave them one of his slaves.

Another day, some children caught a hawk. The young man pleaded with them to set it free, and gave them his second slave. They freed the hawk and it flew away.

When the people caught a mouse, the young man took his remaining, very small slave-girl and gave her to them to let the mouse go. They set it free and the mouse ran away.

From that day, the people thought the young man was mad. He took his spear and walked away into the wilderness. After some time, he became tired and sat down under a tree, just off the path. Suddenly, he heard something that sounded like the roaring of the wind from far, far away; and slowly, slowly a huge snake came crawling towards him. In front of the young man, she curled herself into three large coils and her wattles glowed as red as fire. She looked at him, he looked at her. Then she uncoiled herself and slowly, slowly crawled away.

The young man got up and went on his way. After a few steps, he met another youth sitting quite by himself next to the path.

'Where are you going?' asked the youth.

'I am going to seek my fortune,' answered the young man.

'Whilst you were resting over there, did you see anybody?'

'I met a snake,' replied the young man.

'That was I,' said the youth. 'I am the snake that made the people gather together, in order to kill me; but you said, "Don't kill her." Come with me! One good turn deserves another.'

The young man followed the snake, and when they came to an ant-hill the snake said: 'Hold on to my feet; don't be afraid.'

The young man held on to the snake, and they crawled through a hole in the ant-hill. At last they came to a large town. The guards at the gates did not want to let them pass, but the snake drove them away, and went with the young man into the town and straight to the palace of the Lami'do.

After they had saluted the ruler, the snake said to him: 'When the people wanted to kill me, this young man bought my freedom.' The Lami'do replied that they were his guests, and they were well looked after.

Seven days the young man stayed in that town; then he said that he felt restless and wanted to go home.

'If we go to the Lami'do,' said the snake, 'he will offer you many wonderful presents. Don't accept them. Ask only for the ring on his thumb.'

The young man went and took leave of the Lami'do, who offered him thousands upon thousands of beautiful presents, in fact the whole world. But the young man refused.

'I don't want all that,' he said, 'only the ring on your thumb.'

The king replied: 'But that is such a little thing.'

The young man's only reply was 'Mhm.' So the Lami'do took off his ring and gave it to him.

The snake and the young man left together, but the snake only went with him as far as the spot on the path where they had previously met. Before they said good-bye to each other, the snake said: 'When you reach your sarē, everything you ever wished for in your life will be there.'

And this was all true. When the young man reached home, he found everything in the world, everything he had ever wanted; it was all there in his sarē.

The young man married, but the mother of his wife was a sorceress and was not allowed to live in the village. Her sarē was on the other side of the river. One day, she said to her daughter: 'Get me your husband's ring.'

The daughter, the wife of the young man, took pepper and rubbed it in her eyes so that she could weep without reason. The young man tried to comfort his wife, but she said that all she wanted was the ring on his finger. At last he took the ring off his finger and gave it to her.

She kept it for some time and later gave it to her lover, telling him to take it to her mother on the other side of the river. The lover took it to the mother and she became rich, but the wealth of the young man left him. His wife left him and returned to her mother on the other side of the river.

Poverty came to the young man. He had nothing left at all. He took his staff and walked away once more into the wilderness. Suddenly, the hawk came to him and said: 'Come with me, my friend; I will help you. You once did me a good turn.'

The young man followed the hawk to the hole of the mouse. There the hawk called: 'Crawl out!'

When the mouse came out, the hawk took it in his beak and flew away with it to the sarē of the mother of the young man's wife. There, he dropped the mouse. The mouse gnawed a hole in the pot where the mother kept the ring, took the ring up in his mouth, and crawled out again. Then the hawk picked up the mouse, flew away and dropped it at the feet of the young man. The mouse spat out the ring and returned it to him. They said good-bye to each other, and the young man went home. There all the wealth he had lost came back to him.

The Son of the Lioness and the Son of the Woman

THERE WAS once a young girl, old enough to get married, whose father gave her his trousers and told her to wash them. The girl took them and went down to the river. With legs apart she stood in the swift current and washed the dirty trousers. The water ran between her legs and she conceived by the spirit of the river.

When she became pregnant, her playmates taunted her, saying that her own father had lain with her. The girl became very angry. She took her little gourd, filled it with water and went into the wilderness, right into the middle of the wilderness. There she built herself a little hut and lived in it.

Ashee! There in the wilderness, not far away from the hut of the girl, lived a lioness who had given birth to a cub. Very soon after, the girl gave birth to a son. Every day, before she went out into the wilderness in search of food, the young mother used to rock her child to sleep. One day, the lion cub came and found the child of the young woman. They played together and became great friends, but the lion cub always ran home to his cave just before the mother returned to her child.

This went on until the boy and the cub were grown up. Then one day, the child of the lioness said to his friend: 'You know, my friend, that Allah has so far prevented our mothers from meeting. But should they ever come together in the wilderness, they would fight each other.'

Allah made the lioness and the woman meet one day. The lioness killed the woman and dragged her to the cave. When the cub saw that his mother had killed the woman, the mother of his friend, he refused to eat her flesh. As soon as his mother, the lioness, went out hunting again, the cub ran to his friend and playmate.

'What I feared has happened,' he said. 'Our mothers have met, and yours is dead. But please, don't let that turn your heart against me.'

'It was not your fault,' replied the boy.

Later, when the lioness was out hunting again, her child went to his friend and said:

'Come, let us make a trap and catch my mother and kill her. I, her child, will dig the hole, and you shall carry the earth.'

They dug the trap, and when they had finished it they covered the hole carefully with grass. The lioness returned and, sitting down on the grass, broke through and fell into the trap. The child of the lioness called his friend, the child of the woman, who quickly came to him. Together they filled the hole with earth and buried the lioness.

From that day on the two friends lived together. The cub, who was by now a young lion, did the hunting for food until the boy was fully grown up.

One day, the child of the woman, now nearing manhood, began to worry and grieve.

'I know why you are weeping,' said the lion. 'You would like to go to the village and live there. Well, go to the village. If you see a girl playing with some boys nearing their time for circumcision, make friends with them, and you will also be circumcised.'

The youth did as his friend, the lion, told him, and was circumcised. When he was well again and the festival was due, the lion stole a robe and brought it to his friend in the village. The people of the village adorned and feasted the youth along with their own sons, but as soon as this was over, he went back to his friend, the lion.

A few years passed. The youth was now a man and wanted to marry. The lion said to him:

'It is a black head which, if you hold it against the sun, darkens your day.'

'I will not give you darkness. I promise to do anything you want of me,' replied his friend.

'What I am going to do for you now will enable you to marry. But when you are married, for the sake of our friendship, you must do something for me. Every evening after sunset, I shall come to the back of your sarē and roar. Then you must come out with some butter and rub my back as far as my tail. That will be a sign that you are still fond of me.'

'I promise I will do it,' swore the youth.

'Come along then,' said the lion. 'Let us go to the river where the young girls are bathing, and there you shall point out to me the one you want for a wife.'

The two friends went down to the river where the girls were bathing. Among them was the daughter of the Lami'do. The young man pointed her out to his friend, the lion. The lion leapt and threw himself on the young girl and carried her off.

When the news reached the Lami'do, the people beat the big drum, jumped on horseback and followed the lion. But on seeing the lion, these armed men stood stock still; they were frightened. Then the young man went up to the Lami'do and said:

'I will follow the lion. When I have chased him away, you must give me your daughter in marriage.'

The Lami'do agreed. The young man walked towards the snarling lion, hit him and said: 'Go away.' His friend, the lion, got up and went far away, to the other side of the river.

So it happened that the Lami'do married his daughter to the young man, giving them a sarē and hundreds and hundreds of presents. But every evening, after sunset, the lion came to the back of the sarē of his friend and roared. And at once the young man came out with the butter and rubbed it on the back of the lion as far as his tail.

For a time all went well. But one evening, when he heard the lion roaring, he complained that he was tired of rubbing the lion's back every single night with butter. All the same, he went out with the butter to his friend. Ashee! The lion had heard what he had said, and refused to be touched.

'Take your knife and kill me,' he said.

'You are my friend; I won't kill you,' replied the young man.

'If you don't, I shall kill you,' retorted the lion. So the man, the lion's friend, drew his knife and killed him.

Wounds heal and do not hurt any more, but the stab of a spoken word never heals. Do you understand that?

The Origin of the Bororo

THERE WAS once a pious man, a great sage. He had many, many children, many, many slaves and thousands upon thousands of cattle.

One day, when he was in the hut of his wife saying his prayers, a powerful djinn entered the hut and lay with her. Her husband saw this. From that day on he refused to sleep with her, even though she asked him: 'Why do you refuse yourself to me? Let us sleep together.' But the husband knew that the djinn had lain with his wife, though she herself did not know. She became pregnant, she had conceived by the djinn. So it happened.

After she had given birth to a boy, the djinn returned and lay with her again. And again her husband, the great sage, saw this happen. The woman became pregnant and this time gave birth to a little girl.

Then the sage called all his family and clan together and told them: 'This boy and girl, they will inherit nothing. I did not beget them. I have nine children of my own; to them you will give everything. Those two over there, everybody laughs at them!'

When the father died, the people divided his property among his nine children, but the boy and girl were passed over.

'But I never slept with another man,' protested the mother of these two children.

'Everybody laughs at those two children,' replied her husband's people. The mother wept because her two children inherited nothing.

One day the djinn came to them. He knocked at the back of the hut, called the boy and said:

'Tonight when it is dark, come to the Rabu swamp. There you will find me. I am your father.'

That night, when the boy went to the Rabu swamp, the djinn said to him: 'Call "Hey, hey!", but don't turn round.'

The boy called out: 'Hey, hey!', and out of the swamp rose cattle with large horns. There were so many no one could count them. They started to follow him; but he couldn't help turning round. The cattle sank into the swamp again.

'You will never settle down in a village. You will follow your herds; you will wander about in the bush for all eternity,' were the parting words of the djinn.

From these two children of the djinn come all the clans of the Bororo. That is why they wander through the bush like ghosts. Among them you will not find a single Malum or scribe, because they cannot reason; and that is why their language is a little different from that of the Fulani. The Fulani do not eat with the Bororo, because their marriage customs are uncouth; they have no sarēs in the villages; they only wander about in the bush for ever and ever.

You people of the herds! You Bororos! You are like the restless djinns! As soon as you settle in a village you lose your herds; but there, in the bush, you are the owners of countless herds of cattle.

The Tortoise and the Bush-Child

ONE DAY, the tortoise set out on a journey in search of a child. She met people crushing flies and asked them the way. 'We'll show it to you, but first you must help us with the grinding,' they said.

The tortoise took the round grindstone and helped them. Then they showed her the way. She walked on and met some others grinding bees, gnats and tiny little sand-flies. She asked them the way, and they replied: 'Help us with the grinding and we'll show you the way.'

The tortoise helped them, and they showed her the way. Soon she met herdsmen with cattle. When she asked the way, they said: 'If you bring back our cow which has run away, we'll show you the way.'

She went in search of the cow, found it and brought it back; and the herdsmen saw her on her way.

Next, the tortoise met two pieces of cloth fighting with each other in the middle of the road.

'My dear cloths,' she said, 'please show me the way.'

'Yes, with pleasure,' replied the cloths, 'but first you must separate us, fold us up and put us down.'

She separated the cloths that had been fighting, folded them neatly and put them down, one on one side of the road, and the other on the other side. At once they put her on her way.

For a long time the tortoise walked, until, right in the middle of the middle of the wilderness, she met a maize dumpling boiling away with its sauce and meat. When the tortoise asked it the way, the dumpling replied: 'Only if you stir me, and take and eat as much as you need to satisfy you, will I show you the way.'

She stirred the dumpling, took some of it, poured sauce over it and ate it. Then she washed her hands as a sign that she was satisfied. At once the dumpling showed her the way.

A long, long time the tortoise continued to walk, until at last she came to a village. She went into one of the huts and there she found the bush-child. It had only one eye, one arm, one foot, and its body was dripping with pus. Suddenly, the bush-child said: 'Hi, hi! I want to go into the bush.'

The tortoise put it on her back and started walking. Outside the village the bush-child said: 'Tortoise, dear, please put me down. I didn't want to go into the bush. I only wanted to tell you that the village people are nyam-nyam, man-eaters. They will bring some maize, one single grain of corn, but don't waste your breath arguing about it. Take it and grind it. Later, all the bush animals will come to you, hyenas, leopards, lions and snakes. All of them will come. But don't be frightened; they are only nyam-nyam.'

The tortoise then put the bush-child on her back and carried it home.

In the afternoon the people of the village brought her one single grain of corn, and told her to grind it. The tortoise ground it and gave the flour to the people, who cooked enough porridge to feed the whole village. She went back to her hut.

That night all the animals came to her, hyenas, leopards, lions and snakes. The tortoise was not a bit frightened. She gave them sweet cakes to eat and meat cut up into long, thin strips.

Then she had to go outside. The animals said to her: 'Go, water the cows.' The tortoise made water into the trough and the cows came and drank their fill.

For three days running this happened; then the tortoise said she wanted to go home.

'Hi, hi!' said the bush-child, who was also in the hut. 'I want to go into the bush.'

The tortoise put it on her back and started walking. Outside the village the bush-child said: 'Tortoise, dear, please put me down. I didn't want to go into the bush. I only wanted to tell you that the people will take you into a hut where the pots are stored. Take only three ugly, warped and crooked pots, but none of the good ones.'

The tortoise then put the bush-child on her back again and carried it home.

Later, the people came and took the tortoise to the hut where all the pots were stored. She climbed inside and took three ugly pots, but she also took one of the good ones.

'You must break the pots on your way home,' they told her. As soon as the tortoise was alone in the bush, she broke one of the crooked pots; a little girl was inside. Quickly, she broke the other two; two boys came out of them. There was only the good pot left. She broke it, out jumped a hyena; but the two boys killed the hyena. That is how it happened.

With the three children in front of her, the tortoise walked along the path singing happily:

'Tortoise, you are going home,
Tortoise, you are going home!'

The tarantula in her mud hole heard the singing.

'Tortoise,' she said, 'give me something of what you have there.'

'Blessings on you,' replied the tortoise, 'but whom shall I give you? Who would that leave for me? A'da, the first-born daughter, or my second-born, the dattal-baldana? Or perhaps you will graciously permit me to keep the most trying of the three, the peevish Gaji-am, the youngest?'

Ever since then, the tarantula and the tortoise have been on bad terms. But the tortoise went home with her three children to her swamp, to her rivers.

The Story of the Swamp

ONCE UPON a time there was a woman who had three children, all sons, but she longed to have a little daughter. The woman wept bitterly because she hadn't a little girl.

One day, she suddenly saw a man standing in front of her.

'Why do you weep?' he asked.

She replied that she had three sons but yearned for a little daughter, and this was the cause of her grief.

'Go and pour water over yourself, and wash yourself from head to foot. Then get some chicken eggs and go far into the wilderness, until you reach a swamp with a very large tree growing in the middle of it. Gather some grass, climb up the tree with it and build yourself a nest. Then put the eggs in the nest, sit on them and hatch them out.'

The woman went into the swamp and did exactly as she was told. Her children did not know where she was. For seven days they searched for her everywhere, but they could not find her. At last a hunter saw the woman. There she was, sitting in the tree in the middle of the swamp. He went back to the village and told the children that he had seen their mother.

Next morning, the eldest son drove the cattle to the edge of the swamp. His mother saw him coming and lifted herself up in her nest.

'Drive the cattle back!' she called. 'Turn back or I'll break the eggs! Ashee, ashee! stop, don't come any nearer.' The eldest son turned round and drove the cattle back.

The second-born herded the cattle the next day.

When he came to the place where his brother had been the previous day, once again his mother lifted herself up in the nest and called out: 'My second-born, drive the cattle back! Go back!'

'My mother, mother of us all, I only want to water the herd here among the reeds,' replied her son.

But his mother said: 'Ashee, ashee! Stop, don't come any nearer!'

The second-born, he too, turned round and went away.

On the third day the youngest son came to the swamp with the cattle. Once again his mother called and told him to drive the herd back, but the youngest son refused. He drove the cattle right into the reeds, and they went into the water and drank. But the bull stayed on the bank and roared, stamping on the ground with his hoofs.

An old ox replied to the roaring bull, taunting him: 'All right, all right; we two old and impotent men of the herd!' They began to fight with each other. In the end the bull took the ox on his horns and threw him against the tree, so that the eggs fell out. The woman quickly jumped after them and tried to catch them before they fell into the swamp, but what she caught was a little girl. She held on to the little girl tightly. Putting her on her back, she returned with her son to the village. And so ends this very ancient tale.

All the weeds, the watercress and the ooze of the swamp could not prevent the youngest son from fetching back his mother.

The Evening Star

OF ALL the stars in the sky, there is none so radiant, so beautiful, so clear and so bright as the evening star. If there is no moon among the stars, then the light of the evening star shines like the rays of the moon. She excels above all stars, and that is because she was once a woman; everybody says so.

Long, long ago there lived a man who was clever and peaceful. He was betrothed to a young girl. When she grew to be a woman, there was nobody like her in the whole world, she had become so beautiful. The man married her and they lived together, until one day aversion came and separated them.

The woman said she did not love her husband any longer. The man said: 'So be it; but I still love you.'

Then the little wife ran away; she went right into the very depths of the wilderness. Quite alone, by herself, she went into the wilderness. In the wilderness there was not a single human being.

One day, when she was quite weak with hunger, she sat down under a tree. The animals of the wilderness came, the hyenas, and they killed her. But they did not want to eat her, she was too beautiful. So they dug a hole and buried her. That is how it happened.

A very great war broke out, and spread as far as the wilderness. Among the warriors was a pious man. When he saw the grave, he stopped in front of it and asked: 'Who sleeps here?'

Then her body started to speak, saying: 'It is a woman.'

The pious man said: 'If I pray to Allah, you will wake

up from the sleep of death, and return to your husband's house.'

Her body replied: 'I? I certainly will not return.'

The pious man said: 'I beg you, I beseech you in the name of Allah!' But the woman said that she would never return to her husband, whatever happened.

Then the pious man threatened her: 'Allah will punish you.' And he went away to the wars with the warriors.

Allah used His magic power. He took the beauty of the woman and turned it into a star, and set it up in the Western sky. There it became the best betrothed of the sun. And ever since, up there in the sky, shines her all-surpassing beauty.

But as for the body of the woman, Allah took it and threw it into hell fire. And as for the husband of the woman, the evil spirit fell upon him. He went into the wilderness to search for his wife, and there he still wanders, howling like a madman.

The pious man made a song about the man and his wife:

THE MAN: Lost One, come back to me.
Come, Lost One, return to me.
They beat me at daybreak,
They beat me at sunset,
I am weary, I am weary.

THE PIOUS
MAN: Today he is with us: Leave him in peace.
I nursed him; I beat him;
I beat him; I tore his clothes.

Whatever I do; whatever his fate. If
evening never comes again,
He cannot forget her;
He cannot faint; he does not sleep.
He only sings: 'Lost One, come back to me'.

The Spell

I CLOSE this book with the great cattle spell; there is none
like it in all the world.

He who knows this spell will own many cattle, and
never in his life will he want for cattle hereafter.

> I spit this spell over the book;
> I spit it over Amadu and A'da;
> I spit it over all the Fulani in this world.
>   Fusfa Abadan — for ever and ever!

> Baldheaded spirit of White-faced Cows,
> Master of the milking vessels,
> Master of the watering places,
> Master of the pasture grounds,
> You, who give me my fill to eat,

> Doolo, look after me!
> Doolo, who knows;
> Doolo, who fully knows,
> Give me my fill to eat!

> I have no plenty,
> I have no granary,
> I have no earning,
> I have no cattle pen.

> Doolo, get me cattle,
> Doolo, get me sheep,
> Doolo, get me slaves,
> Doolo, get me slave-children,
> Doolo, get me horses!

I, myself, I get You, Doolo!

Doolo gets cloth – I get cloth,
Doolo gets camels – I get camels,
Doolo gets iron – I get iron,
Doolo gets asses – I get asses.

You, help me, Gontaro!
You, help me, Toringa!
Fill my place with sheep, Fullinga!
Fill it with horses,
Fill it with staples of cloth!

Doolo gets me cattle – I myself get cattle.
My cattle graze at the river,
My cattle are as many as there are people in the town,
As many as there are Djinns at Ja'bam-Tore,
As many as there are people in the world;
My cattle are as many as the drops of water in the big
river.

Cattle I receive!
Give me many sickles to cut grass,
Give me a place of my own!

Get sticks, notch them;
Break them, take them,
Into the tree's fork put them!

Cows, turn round and low,
Sheep, turn round and bleat,
Thus low and bleat with me!

Bull of mine, bellow with me,
Calves of mine, bleat with me,
Unborn calves of mine, bleat with me!

I am the unearthed cloth!
I am Doolo's little Bull!

Spear-carrying Jong-jongle, don't use the spear!

I am the little herdsman of all of You!
I am the first-born son of all of You!
It is I who herd my cattle!

Geyel, you Maker of Forgetfulness,
Malagel Mangel, you Greatest of Djinns,
Let me enjoy my cattle,
No slaughtering, no selling,
Nothing but milking!

Make the milk run as though it came out of a great lake
that never dries!

I shall keep the milk in the chakka-chakk middle of my
hut!

Do not tell this spell to squanderers and ne'er-do-wells;
do not tell it to fools!

If you spit and spell it over your cows, they will
become many, many cows, thousands and thousands,
countless cows.